What the England fast bowlers say…

"Fast-paced, gripping, with a bumper of an ending, *Bowl Like the Devil* is a ripsnorter of a book." **Chris Tremlett**, England fast bowler

"A great read for any aspiring young fast bowler, that makes you realise anything is possible." **Katherine Brunt**, England women's fast bowler

"A helluva story, it gets right inside a fast bowler's head." **Devon Malcolm**, ex-England fast bowler

"A fiendishly good read." **Jonathan Agnew**, ex-England fast bowler

To Bid
and in memory of Fiery Fred

JANETTA OTTER-BARRY BOOKS

Text copyright © Bob Cattell 2012
Illustrations copyright © Keith Sparrow 2012

First published in Great Britain in 2012 by
Frances Lincoln Children's Books,
74-77 White Lion Street, London, N1 9PF

www.franceslincoln.com

A catalogue record for this book is available from the British Library.

ISBN 978-1-84780-282-8

Set in Sabon

Printed and bound by CPI Group (UK) Ltd, Croydon, CR0 4YY

BOWL LIKE THE DEVIL

BOB CATTELL

Illustrations by Keith Sparrow

FRANCES LINCOLN
CHILDREN'S BOOKS

Off Eighteen Paces

It was raining – a sharp April shower – and the grass sparkled like a jewel, as it only ever did in the days just before the cricket season began.

As he peered through the window at the playing fields across the road, in his daydream he saw himself running up to the wicket, leaping into his delivery stride and despatching a ball at 90 miles an hour. It swung late inside the batter's desperate lunge and sent the middle stump cartwheeling across the ground. He smiled to himself.

"Tyrone!" shouted Mr Bluck, his English teacher. "What was I talking about just now?"

Tyrone jumped.

"Er, I... I... was it Shakespeare?"

Two girls at the back giggled. He knew he was in trouble.

"No, it was not Shakespeare," sneered Shorty Bluck. "And since you aren't interested in listening to my lesson, you can find out what you've been missing after school. Understood, Tyrone?"

"Yes, Mr Bluck," whispered Tyrone. He hated the way Blucky said his name with two long, stretched-out syllables. Tye-rown... like he was describing something he'd found on the bottom of his shoe. Staying on after school was a disaster. It meant he would miss net practice. And how was he going to become the fastest bowler in the world if he didn't train properly?

@ @ @

It was nearly six o'clock when Tyrone arrived at the cricket nets at the far end of the playing fields. An hour of writing out a long poem by someone called Ted Hughes hadn't improved his mood.

As expected, he had the nets all to himself – the others would have left ages ago, they never practised for long. He propped up a piece of wood as a wicket against the end of the bedraggled old netting and took a tennis ball wrapped in black tape out of his bag.

His long run-up ended in a stutter and a jerky, ungainly swing of the arm. The ball was propelled in a slow loop into the top corner of the nets and a good two metres from his target.

He picked it up and bowled again. This time it bounced three times and rolled into the opposite corner. His next ball looped straight on to the roof of the nets. Tyrone sighed. It took him a while to retrieve it, jumping up and swinging a stick.

As the ball finally bounced off, he noticed a strange little man watching him from the edge of the nets. He was no more than five foot tall and completely bald with a white goatee beard. He wore no shirt under his crumpled black suit, and a pair of dusty white trainers added to his down-at-heel appearance. But what struck Tyrone most about the diminutive man were his piercing eyes, which seemed to glow a luminous green.

Some weirdo, thought Tyrone, though the

stranger's presence wasn't at all threatening.

"You're pretty crap at that, aren't you?" said the little man, picking up the ball and lobbing it to Tyrone. He had a slight foreign accent. East European, perhaps?

"What do you mean?" stuttered Tyrone, taken aback by the man's direct approach... rude, some would call it.

"I mean your run-up's rubbish, you bowl off the wrong foot, your shoulder's way out of line and your wrist action's all over the place. What's more, you've got no balance, no rhythm and no aggression."

"And apart from that I'm pretty good," said Tyrone, getting his sense of humour back just in time.

The little man smiled. "How would you like to bowl a really fast ball, dead on middle stump? And I mean hurricane fast!"

"Yeah."

"Right, come with me."

The man measured out a run-up of 18 paces. "Three times six, that's the special number," he muttered.

Then he put the ball in Tyrone's hand and turned him to face the plank at the end of the net. "Fix your eyes on your target and, all the time you're running up to the wicket, think: *I'm going to smash it in two*," he said. "Right. Ready, steady, run!"

You feel a huge surge run through your body. Your legs power you towards the bowling crease and as your arm comes over there's an explosion of energy from somewhere deep inside you. The follow-through nearly drags you off your feet, but the ball smacks into the matting and rears up like a striking cobra. There's a loud crack, and the plank trembles and falls to the ground in two halves.

"Not bad. 77 miles an hour," said the voice from behind.

"D...did I do that?" gasped Tyrone.

"Sure did," said the little man. "And you can do it every time if you really want to."

"How?"

"Eighteen paces and then say, *Here's one for Old Nick*. And it helps if you get angry, too."

"Old Nick?"

"That's my name, Nick."

"Oh, mine's Tyrone."

"I know. So there you go, Tyrone, you've got your wish. Fastest, deadliest bowler in the county. And you can get even faster if you want… 90 mph… 100 even, if you want it enough."

"But how? I mean why have you…"

"Why have I helped you? Because I want to. And maybe one day you'll be able to help me."

"How?"

"You needn't worry about that yet. Think about your bowling… we'll talk about the other stuff later."

"What other stuff?" said Tyrone.

But the little man in the black suit was already turning the corner into the car park. Hell, he moves quickly, thought Tyrone.

Just before he disappeared from sight, Nick turned and fixed Tyrone with his piercing eyes. "Remember… 18 paces," he said. Even though he was the other side of the playing field, his voice seemed to come from close by.

Fame At Last

Tyrone wasn't a regular member of the school team. The reason for that, he told himself, was because he didn't get on with the captain, a long-faced, humourless boy named Jim, who picked all his friends for the team even though they were mostly rubbish. But in his heart, Tyrone also knew that he hadn't performed too well whenever he'd been given a chance to play. Jim had let him bowl only three overs the whole of last summer and on each occasion he'd given away loads of runs and even more wides.

As for batting, his highest score ever was nine and he held the school record for ducks – or so Jim and his friends said. He also had a worrying habit of dropping catches, particularly at critical times in the game. Not that there were too many critical times because the team usually lost by a mile and a half. Last year they hadn't won a single game and they'd been bottom of the league ever since Tyrone had been at the school.

As luck would have it, though, a nasty bout of spring 'flu accounted for four of Jim's mates, and so Tyrone was picked for the first game of the season. Since meeting the mysterious Nick, he had tried out his new bowling method a couple of times in the nets, but only when he'd been on his own. There was something about the surge of power and the speed his arm came over that scared him. It was as if someone else was in his body. However, each time he tried it, it worked, and each ball was faster, more accurate and more deadly than the one before.

The more Tyrone thought about the strange encounter with Nick, the more puzzled he became. The questions piled up. How had Nick known his name? Had he used a hidden speed gun to tell him the ball had been fired down at 77 mph, or was he just guessing? But most of all he wondered just where

his new-found, deadly bowling skill had come from
and whether it would last.

◎ ◎ ◎

The first fixture was a home game for St Peter's,
Tyrone's school, against Middleditch who had been
second in the League last year. St Pete's lost the
toss and were put in to bat. Tyrone's best friend,
Cristiano, scored 45 out of a disappointing total of
62. Tyrone batted at 11 and got one not out.

Cristiano was the only truly talented cricketer
in the school team. He was one of those lucky
people who could play any sport – cricket, football,
athletics, tennis – and be brilliant at all of them
without even trying. There was no point in envying
Cristiano. If you asked him how come he batted or
bowled so well without bothering with training, he
would grin and shrug his shoulders. It was almost
as if he didn't care.

Tyrone *did* care: he cared a lot and he would
have given anything to play cricket half as well as
Cristiano. He wanted to win, too. In fact winning

was just about the most important thing in his life.

However, the differences in the ability and character of the two boys hadn't got in the way of them becoming friends. Living in the same street, they'd known each other for years. Their families were close and last year they'd gone on holiday together. At school Tyrone and Cristiano were inseparable and in the evening they'd walk home talking about cricket and football and why their teachers were so weird.

Jim didn't like Cristiano. He was deeply jealous of his talent, and he made it as difficult as possible for Cristiano to play a starring role for the team by bowling him at the wrong time or batting him down the order when the game was already lost. Cristiano didn't seem to notice any of this: he'd just shrug when Tyrone complained about Jim's favouritism or his hopeless captaincy. But Tyrone noticed everything... and Jim knew it.

The umpires marched out for the start of the Middleditch innings followed by the St Peter's Xl, who straggled out on to the field looking more like a bunch of young convicts than a cricket team.

Jim chose two of his mates to open the bowling, even though they were nowhere near as good as Cristiano and, after six overs of horrible trash, Middleditch had scored 34 for no wicket.

"Another glorious defeat," said Cristiano to Tyrone breezily, as they passed each other at the end of the over.

"Will he ever give you a bowl?" said Tyrone urgently.

Cristiano grinned. "Make no difference now. It's too late… even if I took a hat trick. Perhaps he'll bring you on instead."

"Erm… I'm not sure I want to bowl today," said Tyrone.

"Why not, for heaven's sake?"

"Well, my shoulder's a bit sore. Maybe I've been practising too much."

Jim finally gave Cristiano a bowl from the pavilion end and he immediately took two wickets with his off-breaks. Cristiano, of course, could bowl anything he liked: off-breaks or leg-breaks, seam or swing. He'd chosen his off-breaks today and he was turning the ball a mile. After two overs

Jim took him off.

Only two more wickets fell in the next half hour, one of them to a fine running catch on the boundary by Cristiano. But three other catches were dropped and, by now, the Middleditch opener was on the verge of steering his team to an easy victory. They were 57 for four.

"You may as well have the last over," Jim said to Tyrone with a smirk. *Last over!* Tyrone would have told him to get stuffed if he hadn't just overheard Jim talking to one of his mates. "We're going to lose, so we might as well have a laugh and watch Ty make a fool of himself."

We'll see who's the fool, thought Tyrone angrily.

He marked out his run-up – precisely 18 strides – shot a sour look at Jim in the slip cordon and fixed his eyes on the wicket. The tall opener watched with awakening alarm as the bowler ran in.

Here's one for Old Nick. The energy runs through you like an electric shock. You explode into the final stride and unleash an unstoppable missile.

The Middleditch player hardly has time to raise his bat before he hears the crash behind him and two out of the three stumps are ripped out of the ground and sent wheeling towards the keeper. The batter opens his mouth to say something. He inspects what's left of his wicket. You know he didn't even see the ball as it whistled past him. You punch the air. Take that, skipper!

There was a deathly silence. And then Cristiano came rushing up to congratulate his friend.

"I don't know how you did that... but it was truly amazing, Ty," he said, giving his friend a broad grin and punching knuckles triumphantly.

"Just luck," said Tyrone quietly. "It seemed to come out right, though."

"It's the fastest ball I've ever seen anyone bowl," said Cristiano. "Can you do it again?"

"Dunno. I'll try." Tyrone noticed that Jim and his friends hadn't come over to speak to him but they were huddled together, casting strange looks in his direction. He stood at the end of his run-up waiting for the next batter. It was the Middleditch captain. He took a while to take his guard, looking about the field arrogantly, as if to say, I'll soon finish off this lot.

I'll fix him, you think... Here's one for Old Nick... and you storm in again off the 18-pace run-up, driven forward by that strange new force. This time the ball swings in viciously at pace, almost cutting the batter in two. He makes a despairing lunge at it with his bat, nearly sweeping himself off his feet before staring back forlornly at the wreckage of his wicket.

"Brilliant!" shouted Cristiano. "One more for the hat trick."

Tyrone smiled. All the anger had drained out of him and he took the ball again. I'll see if I can do it without the *Old Nick* thing, he thought to himself... a fast yorker on middle stump, that should fix him. But as soon as he started running in he knew it was going all wrong.

The batter, all tensed up for another thunderbolt, couldn't believe his luck. The ball was short and slow and sat up invitingly and he swung it away gratefully for four.

"They only need two to win now," said Jim, handing the ball back to his bowler.

From the tone of his voice Tyrone could tell he was relaxing a bit after the shock of the first two balls. Another rubbish ball and hand victory to the opposition... that's what would make Jim happy. Of course, he couldn't say it outright, but the last thing he wanted was for Tyrone to transform himself into a fast-bowling hero.

Tyrone stared coldly at his captain before carefully marking out his run-up again. "Just watch this, mate," he said under his breath.

The first ball of the hat trick detonated the middle stump. The second was plumb lbw and so fast that, as it thudded into the batter's pad, he yelped in pain. The third thwacked the off-stump half-way up and it snapped in two, sending the bails flying high in the air.

Suddenly the score was 61 for nine and the Middleditch number 11 remembered that he'd hurt his back and couldn't bat. Victory was handed to

St Peter's. Their first victory in over two years!

Even Jim managed to join in the generous applause for Tyrone as he led the team off the field. His bowling figures were: one over, five wickets for four runs.

Cristiano could hardly contain himself. "Just wait till I tell Dad," he kept saying, beaming broadly all the time. "He's not going to believe it."

Enter God

That was the beginning of a summer that Tyrone would never forget. The news of the great victory blazed through the school like wildfire. Everyone wanted to talk to Tyrone. Even the older boys and teachers, who before had scarcely acknowledged his existence, queued up to hear the story. Mr Bennett, the head teacher, paraded him in front of the whole school in assembly and said that Tyrone was an example to them all about how hard work and practice can pay off... which just showed how much he knew.

Of course, everyone wanted to see Tyrone bowl. After-school net practice became so crowded that they were standing on boxes and climbing trees to get a glimpse of the school's new star pace bowler in action. Tyrone didn't want to disappoint. So, whenever he had an audience, he abandoned his normal way of bowling and used the *Old Nick* method. And it never failed.

Being the most popular boy in the school was a completely novel experience for Tyrone. People pointed him out to their parents, teachers smiled and talked to him between lessons and Jim Davy, the PE teacher, never stopped holding him up as an example to all the others in the class. And Tyrone started to enjoy being the centre of attention.

◎ ◎ ◎

It was more than three weeks before he saw Nick again. By then St Peter's had won their next two games by a landslide and were top of the league. Cristiano had scored most of the runs and Tyrone had taken seven wickets in the first game and nine in the second. There wasn't a player around who could lay a bat on him.

He was taking his dog, Boomer, for a walk by

the river when Nick appeared at his side…as if from nowhere. It scared the life out of Boomer, who shot off through a hedge barking like crazy and didn't return home till much later that evening. That was strange in itself… because Boomer was never one to back out of a fight, especially with dogs two or three times his size, and he had a nasty habit of taking a bite out of their owners, too. Tyrone had never seen Boomer run away from anything before.

"Sorry, I sometimes have that effect on animals," said Nick. "Been playing any cricket?"

"Yeah," said Tyrone. "And what I want to know is…"

"You're too good for that school team, you know."

"What d'you mean?"

"Time you were playing on the big stage. Proper club cricket and county level stuff."

"And how am I supposed to do that, I don't know any…"

"It's all sorted. The County coach came to see you play last week. You'll get a letter from someone tomorrow."

"How do you know?"

Nick grinned. "Not much I don't know... you'll see."

"Then tell me what's going on... with my bowling, I mean? What have you done to make me bowl so fast?"

"It's what you've done," said Nick. "You're a good listener and you're ambitious. If you keep listening you'll be the most famous bowler in the world one day. Isn't that what you want?"

"Well... yes."

"Another little trick for you, then," said Nick, producing a cricket ball from the pocket of his black jacket like a magician pulling a rabbit out of a hat. He held the ball with the seam running between his long bony fingers. "Hold it like this and it'll swing away at the last second towards the slips."

He twisted the ball in his grip so that the seam ran the other way, across the top joints of his fingers. "And this will give you really wicked bounce. Nothing like a good bouncer to keep those batters on their toes." He chuckled and then his face suddenly turned stony serious. "So what are you going to give me then?" he demanded.

"Give you?"

"Well, you don't think I'm doing it for nothing?"

"You mean money?"

"Perhaps."

Tyrone thought for a moment. "My next week's pocket money, then," he said.

"What, two quid? Is that all?" said Nick, his eyes narrowing a little more.

"How'd you know..." began Tyrone.

"Couldn't you steal some?" said Nick.

"No," said Tyrone defiantly. He'd never stolen anything in his life.

"Your mum wouldn't miss a few quid."

Tyrone stared at him, aghast.

"Oh, all right...only joking," said Nick with an exaggerated smile. "Two pounds it is." And in the wink of an eye he was gone, ducking down a side path into the undergrowth.

"See you next week, there's more where that came from," said a voice in Tyrone's ear.

The letter Nick had promised duly arrived in the next morning's post. It was from someone called Godfrey Boddy at the County Ground and offered Tyrone an immediate trial with the County Colts.

Godfrey Boddy turned out to be a thick-set, middle-aged man, dapper in a county tie and blazer. He had a shaved head, big, bushy eyebrows that joined in the middle and tufts of hair growing out of his ears. He welcomed Tyrone to the County Ground like a favourite son and didn't let him out of his sight for a second until the trial game began.

Mr Boddy, known as *God*, short for Godfrey, to all and sundry, told him with a stage wink, that he was 'the laddy in charge of youth development and one or two other things around here'. He'd certainly done his homework on Tyrone's early-season performances and talked with relish about each of the recent wickets the young quick bowler had taken.

The trial match began sensationally with Tyrone taking three wickets in his first over. The opposition were bowled out for 23. Tyrone's contribution was seven wickets for five runs. The game was all over by tea-time and, before he left the ground, Tyrone had been signed up to play not only his first game for the County Colts but also for Vale of Eden CC, one of the top clubs in the county, whose chairman was... guess who? None other than *God* himself.

Tyrone and Cristiano met that evening. Tyrone was bursting to tell his friend about his sensational day, but Cristiano was strangely quiet and didn't seem to be in the mood to listen. Tyrone's latest tales of his bowling triumphs were met with a stony silence.

Eventually Cristiano let him know what was on his mind. "So you've walked out on St Pete's, have you, Ty?"

"Well, you have to admit it's a rubbish team... and Jim's a joke captain," said Tyrone.

"I thought we were having fun."

"But I want to play proper cricket not fun cricket."

"So you think you're too good for us now, do you?"

"What do you think?"

"Don't ask me, Ty," said Cristiano, with a shrug.

"When you were bowling rubbish I always tried to get Jim to find a place for you in the team. Now that you're suddenly the great star fast bowler and we've started winning a few games for a change, you tell me you're leaving."

"But I need to play top-level cricket if I'm going to become…"

"Become what?" demanded Cristiano. "Become a mega-star? Bowl for the County? Become the great England fast bowler? Better than Stuart Broad? Better than Jimmy Anderson? Is that what you think, Ty?"

"Well… er… look, I just want to keep improving my game. You could easily play for the Colts too, if you…"

"Improving your game? Don't make me laugh. A few weeks ago you couldn't bowl fast and straight if I'd offered you a million quid. Now you're the deadliest, fastest bowler any of us have ever seen. How did that happen, eh? You didn't *improve,* you changed overnight. So, tell me, who taught you to do that?"

"No one!" insisted Tyrone. "It just started

coming out right. No one taught me."

"Why don't I believe you?" said Cristiano slowly.

"You calling me a liar?"

"I'm just saying something happened. You're different, Ty. You've changed. And I'm not just talking about your bowling."

"Well maybe it's a good thing I've changed." Tyrone felt the anger burning inside him. If he'd been bowling a cricket ball it would probably have broken the 100mph speed record. "I can't help it if you've got no ambition and want to go on playing for a Mickey Mouse team. But I'm not like that. I want something better. I want to get to the top. I want to win."

Cristiano stared at him. Tyrone didn't know whether he was going to hit him or burst into tears. Then, with a shrug of the shoulders, his best friend turned and walked away. "Go to the devil!" were the last words Tyrone heard him say.

Vale of Eden

And they *were* Cristiano's last words to Tyrone...
for some time, at least. Because, after their row, the
two erstwhile friends contrived a big freeze. For two
whole weeks they shunned each other at school.
They crossed the road to avoid meeting. One would
walk out of the corner shop without a word if the
other came in. And then fate took a hand. Cristiano's
dad got a new job. His parents moved across the
county, nearly 20 miles away, and Cristiano went to
another school.

To begin with, Tyrone told himself that losing
his best friend wasn't that big a deal, especially
since he wasn't his best friend any more. But as
soon as Cristiano's family moved, he realised just

how much he missed his friend. Cristiano had been the only person he'd ever really trusted...apart from his mum, of course. She told him not to worry: the families would get together at weekends and they would go on holiday again in August.

Nevertheless, his mother was a little alarmed by Tyrone's recent behaviour and utterly perplexed by her son's fast-bowling obsession and his rocketing success. She told herself it was probably because she didn't understand the first thing about cricket, but she also had a sneaking feeling that Tyrone was hiding something from her.

"How are you getting on with Mr Boddy?" she asked him one day.

"Fine," he said, without looking up.

"Are you sure you're not being persuaded to play too much cricket? I mean, there are other things in life...not to mention your school work."

"Of course I want to play cricket," insisted Tyrone. "And who says I'm not working at school?"

"No one yet," said his mother. "But I hope you'll tell me if things are getting difficult for you. You've always shared things with me, haven't you?"

Tyrone nodded and looked away.

@ @ @

Meanwhile, Tyrone's fame on the cricket field continued to grow rapidly under the watchful eye of Godfrey Boddy. The new fast-bowling prodigy starred in a succession of victories for both the County Colts and his new club, Vale of Eden. People began to point him out in the street and he'd hear other players talking about him in hushed whispers. He noticed too the look of fear in the eyes of the opposing teams' batters. Word got around quickly!

His team mates were only too happy to bathe in the reflected glory that Tyrone brought them. They slapped him on the back and punched knuckles as each wicket fell; they cheered him off the ground after every victory; they grinned at him, high-fived him, praised him and flattered him.

The Vale of Eden captain, Simon, was the crawliest of the flatterers. He sidled up to Tyrone at the start of each game and asked him where

he wanted his fielders placed, how many overs he wanted to bowl and which end he wanted to bowl from. It was all a bit creepy.

But although Tyrone got all the attention in the world, he never made any real friends amongst his fellow players....

God was partly responsible for this because he kept a constant eye on Tyrone and insisted on whisking him away from the ground as soon as stumps were drawn. "Come on, laddy," he would say. "I promised your mother I'd ferry you home promptly." Which was kind of strange because Tyrone knew his mum never worried about him being out late, and anyway she would have been perfectly happy to pick him up after the games herself.

But *God* insisted that it was his duty. "We need to keep your boy away from the sharks," he told Tyrone's mother by way of justification, though neither she nor Tyrone understood which *sharks* he meant or where they were to be found.

On their car journeys, criss-crossing the county to and from games, Godfrey Boddy kept up a never-ending commentary on his plans for Tyrone's future. "We'll have you playing in the County Under-15s next year," he'd say. "And who'd bet on it that you won't soon be picked for the England elite squad? The scouts have been watching... and I know them well. They all dream about spotting the next great fast bowler, because fast bowlers are different and the great ones only come along once in a lifetime."

There was no doubt about Godfey Boddy's ambitions for Tyrone. But something about his methods left Tyrone feeling a trifle uneasy. It came out in the way he drove his powerful BMW across the countryside, swearing at any driver or cyclist or pedestrian who dared to get in his way. And then there were the things people said about him... not all of them complimentary. In praising *God* one day, Old Nick seemed to sum it up.

"Godfrey's what I'd call a first-class fixer," he said.

"What do you mean?"

"Let's just say he gets his own way. Godfrey is only interested in one thing: and that's winning. And he doesn't much mind how he wins."

"You don't make him sound very nice."

"Nice? What's nice got to do with it?" Nick's eyes flashed. "Just you listen to what he says and he'll take you to the top. That's what you want, isn't it?"

"Well...yes."

This exchange took place behind a large display of baked beans at Sainsbury's, where Nick had performed his latest appearing trick and where Tyrone was doing some reluctant last-minute shopping for his mum.

Nick had stood by his promise lately of regularly supplying Tyrone with a succession of killer deliveries for his fast-bowling armoury. Now each delivery had a scary name such as the *Toe Cruncher* and the *Throat Ball* and the *Mean Missile* and the *Cannonball*, and they fully lived up to their deadly titles. The only trouble was that all Tyrone's pocket money was disappearing as fast as the batters who faced his bowling. And Nick seemed to want more and more money before sharing his secrets.

Today he got to the point straight away. "You want me to show you how to bowl a *Fizzer*? Scares the living daylight out of them, does a *Fizzer*."

"Yes, please."

"Got any money for me?"

"No. I've spent all my pocket money."

"Then how are you going to pay for the shopping?"

Tyrone pulled a twenty-pound note out of his pocket and Nick snatched it.

"You can't have that, it's my mum's," said Tyrone.

"Tell her you lost it. Or better still, you could do a runner with the shopping and tell her nothing."

"But..." began Tyrone.

"I'll show you the *Fizzer* next time," said Nick, turning the corner into the next aisle and disappearing from sight. He left Tyrone frozen to the spot, not knowing what to do next.

Jez

In the end, he decided to lie to his mum rather than steal from the supermarket. Tyrone would have preferred stealing to lying but he was too scared of getting caught. And there was no way he could tell his mum about Old Nick, so what choice did he have? His mum was angry about him losing the twenty pounds but she soon got over it.

Old Nick was true to his word. The following week he 'materialised' as Tyrone was walking home from school and taught him the *Fizzer*. He seemed quite annoyed that Tyrone hadn't taken the thieving option. "The supermarket can afford it more than your mum can. Think about that next time," he said.

Tyrone didn't like sound of 'next time', but he quickly put the thought out of his head and concentrated on the *Fizzer*. And soon the nasty, shooting and scuttling delivery was hammering into the toes and ankles of batters across the county.

It was around this time too that Tyrone started experimenting with *getting angry*. The angrier he got the faster he could bowl. So he looked out for things, especially about the batter at the other end of the strip, to make him angry. Soon he was able to work himself into a rage at just the way his opponent took guard, or walked out to tap down the pitch, or fidgeted at the crease. He enjoyed the way the anger allowed him to bowl a yard faster. And slowly his anger turned into a sort of blind hatred of all batters.

@ @ @

Tyrone wasn't the only cricketer to attract the attention of the County scouts that season. There was another young batter who had taken the junior league by storm, demolishing all previous records in the process: *three centuries in succession, youngest batter to score 150, top of the County averages by a country mile with an amazing 99.94, fastest 50 ever!*

The name of this phenomenon was Jezebel... or Jez for short. She played for Jericho Hall, over the other side of the county from Vale of Eden. Her dad was a useful club cricketer, an all-rounder., who opened the bowling for Jericho Hall's First XI and batted at six.

Even as a young child, before she went to school, Jez had begged her father to bowl at her in the garden. Her older brother was more interested in football, but Jez would be waiting every evening with her tiny cricket bat for her father to come home from work. And it didn't take him long to realise he had a prodigy on his hands.

The cover drive came naturally to Jez and she was hooking and pulling before she learned to play her immaculate backward and forward defensive shots. But it was her footwork and the amount of time she seemed to have to play her shots which singled Jez out from the other talented players.

Later, all the bowlers she faced would be driven crazy by her uncanny knack of picking the length of a ball almost before it left the hand. "It's like she was reading my mind," one bowler said, after a terrible mauling as Jez raced to one of her stylish centuries.

To begin with, her father was careful about rushing her into competitive games, but Jez, as usual, took things in her stride. By the age of eight she was playing every sort of cricket available to her: Kwik cricket at school, net practice three times a week with the club and regular matches for the under-11s with players twice her size. She even got a few games with the local pub team when they were short, which seemed to happen most weeks of the summer. And if she wasn't playing cricket she'd take on the job of scoring for the first XI.

Jez was also blessed with a remarkable temperament. Nothing phased her. When she got out to a good ball, she would nod her approval at the bowler and walk off. When she got a bad decision, she'd never argue with the umpire or throw a tantrum in the changing room like some of the *prima donnas* in the team. She was also mentally tough and her body language told everyone in the opposing team that she was in charge.

One game, played when she was only ten, summed up her ability and growing maturity. Jericho Hall Juniors were facing their biggest test of the season in an away game against the club's old foe, Southwell Saints. Everything went wrong for the Jerichos from the start. Their opening fast bowler limped off with a side strain after bowling three balls and then they dropped six catches and missed three easy run-out chances. The Saints managed to get to a total of 114 off 20 overs on a pitch that was really helping the seamers.

The mood in the changing room between innings was poisonous: everyone was blaming someone else for their performance. Jez sat next to her friend Harriet, who was a year older than her and the only other girl in the team. She let the boys moan on and then said quietly, "114. We can knock them off, can't we?"

Jericho Hall's innings continued the disaster. Three wickets fell in the first over. Then, after a brief recovery, Saints' fastest bowler came back and took a wicket with the first ball of his new spell and a hat trick off the last three balls of the over. 33 for seven.

Jez had watched the three wickets fall from the other end. She had faced one ball only and taken a single off it. She was now joined by Harriet, a bowler who could bat a bit. "I'll keep the strike for a couple of overs," said Jez, taking charge. "If you have to face, just block it."

The next three balls went four…four…four. After the third boundary, a sweet cover drive dissecting the field, the Saints players were looking at each other nervously. The victorious mood had changed a little. Jez blocked the next ball, lifted the fifth of the over expertly over the single slip for four more and ran a single off the last.

She was now facing the tall quickie who had done all the damage – taking six of the seven wickets. He came in off a long run-up and bowled a vicious bouncer that reared up from only just short of a length. Jez took it on and hooked. The ball flew off the middle of her bat and sailed over the

deep square-leg boundary for six. She then flicked a yorker off her toes for four and drove another majestic cover drive through the field.

By the end of the over, Jericho Hall's total had doubled to 66… but Jez had lost the strike. Harriet fell to the third ball she faced and the number 10 missed two balls and then was clean bowled. They were 66 for nine. Jez had a brief chat with Archie, Jericho's last batter. She knew Archie had only one shot…the slog – usually played with his eyes shut.

And she'd learnt her lesson well. For four overs Archie didn't face a ball. Jez put away all the bad deliveries. If the ball didn't reach the boundary they ran two. And she expertly picked the gap in the field to take a single off the last ball of the over. The score mounted rapidly…80…90…. The 100 came up with a perfectly timed sweep shot off the spinner. The Saints were now beginning to panic: their fielding had become ragged and they had given away loads of overthrows. Two more boundaries and a two and the target was in sight. Jez took the single off the last ball and then looked down the wicket in horror to see Archie coming back for a second run.

There was nothing for it but to run...she dived and beat the throw by a couple of inches.

But now she was at the wrong end. 112 for nine. Only three runs to win. She couldn't bear to think of throwing it away at the last hurdle.

"If it's not on the stumps, swing and try and get some bat on it," she told Archie calmly, but feeling rather desperate.

The field closed in as the Saints sensed victory again. The bowler grunted as the ball left his hand and Archie played his only shot, like a shot putter's final heave. He missed. The ball flew over the middle stump and everyone on the field groaned except Archie and Jez.

She walked down the wicket again. "Good try. Hit it next time," she said with a reassuring grin.

The next ball came down bang on middle stump. Archie closed his eyes and mowed. With a crack, the ball soared over mid-wicket and bounced twice before it cleared the boundary. Jez was already at the other end congratulating him. She'd won the game single-handed, yet there she was, giving him the hero's treatment.

Twenty20

Vale of Eden CC and Jericho Hall CC had never met before because they were in completely separate leagues at different ends of the county. Tyrone had heard a few stories of Jez's triumphs with the County Juniors, but at county level there were no mixed sides and he didn't take much notice of girls' cricket. He'd never seen her bat. And he probably never would have… if it hadn't been for *God*.

Godfrey Boddy talked quite a bit about Jez as he and Tyrone were driving to and from matches. He didn't appear to have a very high opinion of 'a girl playing in a boys' team', as he called it.

"All very well, girls playing cricket," he'd say. "But we can't have them facing proper fast bowling.

That young lady's going to get seriously hurt one day…mark my words."

But, although Godfrey didn't approve, he didn't let his scruples get in the way of his plotting. And the *Godfrey Boddy Twenty20 Junior Tournament* was his latest plan.

He had looked down his nose at Twenty20 cricket when it first started. "Call that cricket! It's just biff and baff." He'd say it over and over again… to anyone who sought his views on the subject. But the moment he saw that this new form of the game was going to be a big crowd-puller, everything changed.

The *Godfrey Boddy Twenty20 Junior Tournament* quickly established itself over the season with most of the County League teams competing. The Tournament Final was billed as one of the star evening attractions of County Cricket Week. And Godfrey knew full well what the outcome of all his plotting was likely to be.

Sure enough…Vale of Eden and Jericho Hall, both unbeaten all season, finished top of their respective Twenty20 leagues and won through to the final of the competition. And when this happened,

God wasn't slow to promote the game as the clash between Tyrone, the fastest young bowler in the county, and Jez, the great new batting prodigy.

As Cricket Week approached, *God* gave Tyrone plenty of tips on how to bowl at Jez. He seemed to have set aside all his concerns for her safety.

"You can't give her an easy time just because she's a girl," he said. "She's the one who wants to play a man's game. Let her take the consequences. Bouncers, lifters, they're all part of the quick's armoury... so use them. Get stuck in...understand?"

Tyrone wasn't much bothered. He knew if he did the 18-steps trick and said *Here's one for Old Nick,* the delivery would be unplayable by any batter, let alone a girl.

Then, a week before the final, after a midweek County Colts game – another easy victory by 60 runs – he got a big surprise. As he passed the notice board by the bar he spotted a poster headed *The Godfrey Boddy Twenty20 Junior Tournament.* There were two photos on the poster: Jez playing a hook shot, and one of him bowling. He'd never seen the picture before. *God* must have taken it,

he supposed, though he'd said nothing about it, nor told Tyrone that he was going to use it for the poster.

Underneath the photos were the team sheets for the final. He sought out his own name: there he was… down to bat at 11, as usual, for the Vale. And then he looked at the Jericho Hall team. Jez was batting at 3. But it was the fourth name, underneath hers, that made Tyrone's heart skip a beat.

CRISTIANO!

Cristiano playing for Jericho Hall. Tyrone would be up against his old friend next week!

Cristiano Bowls

A hot August day had turned into a sultry evening. Godfrey Boddy drove Tyrone through the ornate, wrought-iron gates of the county ground.

"I've told young Simon to bat if he wins the toss," said *God* to Tyrone. "I said, get a score on the board first, then Tyrone can bowl them out."

Tyrone nodded. He nodded a lot when Godfrey was about – there wasn't much else you could do.

"Of course, the trouble is you've only got four overs to dispatch them in Twenty20. But that should be more than enough, the way you're bowling, laddie," *God* added.

It was true that Tyrone's bowling record in the Twenty20 tournament had been every bit as devastating as in the regular league games. His best haul had been nine wickets and he had three more five-fors to his credit.

Old Nick had taught him a few extra 'specials' for the twenty-over game. He told him he'd be *expecting payment on the night*, which was ominous, because Tyrone had no money. One of the 'specials' was a wickedly disguised slower ball. It was actually a slow full-toss but all the batters took it for a fast beamer aimed straight at their heads. So they ducked or dived out of the way, only to look ridiculous as the ball lobbed gently into their stumps while they grovelled on the ground.

The county ground was a picture. Handsome, striped tents – serving food and drink for the spectators – formed a semi-circle at the top end of the oval-shaped pitch. The pavilion was packed. It was the biggest crowd Tyrone had ever seen at a cricket game.

Simon won the toss and elected to bat, as instructed. Tyrone didn't spot Cristiano until the Jericho Hall team took to the field. He saw his old friend glance over in his direction. There was no expression of surprise. Cristiano obviously knew Tyrone was playing and, like the other Jericho Hall players, he was probably quaking in his shoes at the thought of facing the demon fast bowler.

But if Jez was quaking, she showed no sign of it. She threw catches to her team-mates, shouted words of encouragement, jumped athletically about and did some alarming stretching exercises – everything about her said that she was 100% focused on the game.

She was smaller than Tyrone had expected. She had short, straight hair and a nose which was on the big side...though not that big. In fact Tyrone had to admit she was quite pretty.

The game began well for Vale of Eden. 15 came from the first two overs. But then Cristiano came into the attack and disaster struck. He was bowling his lively in-cutters and both batters found it really hard to get them away. Three in-duckers in a row... then one nipped back the other way, and the opener snicked a low, difficult chance to Jez in the slips.

She dived, snatched the ball at ankle height and never looked like dropping it. As she threw it up in celebration, Tyrone felt a reassuring surge of anger towards her.

The very next ball thudded into captain Simon's pads and he too was sent on his way by the umpire. Cristiano took three wickets in a two-over spell before being rested. After that the Vale of Eden innings struggled to pick up momentum.

They'd limped to 41 for six after ten overs when Godfey Boddy came strolling past the bench where Tyrone was sitting. "That young seam bowler looks fairly useful," he said to Tyrone. "Ever come across him before?"

"We used to play together once," said Tyrone hesitantly

"What's his name?"

"Cristiano. He's not a bad bat either."

At that very moment the ball was skied in the direction of the mid-wicket boundary. It looked like a six but Cristiano ran round the boundary and timed his leap to perfection, plucking a stunning full-stretch chance with the fingertips of his right hand.

"Can catch a bit, too," chortled *God*. "Well caught, lad."

Tyrone and Cristiano found themselves standing almost face to face on the boundary. Neither said a word.

Before long, the last man was walking out to bat. Tyrone had watched Vale of Eden stutter and stumble to 64 for nine and now it was his turn.

The last batter had been clean-bowled by Cristiano, who had just returned to the attack. Tyrone took guard and looked up to see his old friend running in purposefully. The ball pitched on a length and reared up savagely. The crunching blow full on his protective box made Tyrone wince. He bent double and waited for the pain. When it came, he fell to his knees, the breath knocked out of him. A couple of players laughed: someone always did when a batter got one in the goolies. But it was more in sympathy than mockery: everyone knew how much it hurt.

"You OK, Ty?" said Cristiano, who had followed through the full length of the pitch.

Tyrone didn't give him the satisfaction of a reply. He dragged himself to his feet, somehow overcoming the terrible agony in the pit of his stomach, and took guard, tapping his bat impatiently in the crease as if to say, *Come on, you amateurs, I'm waiting*.

A black anger descended over him. If he'd been bowling, the batter would have been in mortal danger.

Cristiano shrugged, took the ball and strode back to his mark. This time the delivery was too

short and Tyrone got a lucky edge. The ball flew away for three streaky runs. Cristiano sank to his knees, holding his head in his hands in frustration. Tyrone smirked.

End of the over and Tyrone was facing again. The new bowler was a spinner. He didn't like spinners. He was always getting out to them.

"Come on, Dominic, finish them off," said the keeper, adding under his breath – but loud enough for Tyrone to hear – "Anyone can see this idiot can't bat."

Without the searing pain in his groin Tyrone might have been amused by the sledging but once again he felt a surge of anger. The keeper was really annoying him.

The first ball looped up on a length. Tyrone got lucky and middled an agricultural heave. It flew high over square-leg for six. He stared hard at the wicket-keeper, who stared back and said, "Bet you can't do that again." He grinned cheekily.

Tyrone tried to repeat the shot to the next ball and it flew off a top edge and rose high into the summer sky. Jez stood under it at mid-on. She waited and waited and waited and the ball fell... faster and faster...straight into her cupped hands. She casually put it her pocket and walked off. Vale were all out for 73.

Tyrone made his way slowly towards the pavilion, keeping out of range of Cristiano and the chirpy wicket-keeper. He was quite pleased with his innings, especially the six, but the raw pain in his lower abdomen was making him feel really bad-tempered. He was half pleased about that too, because he knew he was about to bowl.

The Watching Game

Tyrone took off his pads and gloves in the changing room and, without speaking to anyone, went out for some fresh air. As he rounded the corner of the pavilion he literally bumped into Old Nick.

"Got you where it hurts, did they?" said Nick. "Never mind, you'll make them pay for it."

"You bet."

"The girl can bat, mind. She'll try and take you on," said Nick.

"Let her try."

Nick stroked his wispy beard. "Just as well to have something up your sleeve, though. I could show you the deadliest ball ever bowled, if you like."

"Well..." began Tyrone. He guessed what was coming next.

"Of course, it'll cost you. You got any money with you?"

"No."

"I see. And what about payment for those 'specials' I gave you last week?"

"But you didn't say..."

"Well, I'm saying it now. It's settle-up time, Tyrone." There was a cold steeliness in Nick's voice that Tyrone hadn't detected before.

Tyrone looked at him. His midriff gave him another sharp twinge.

"All right, let's call it thirty quid for the lot. Ten pounds you already owe me, and another twenty for the most wicked ball you've ever bowled. You could nick it from the umpires' pockets in their changing room. There's thirty quid in the trousers hanging on the left and the door's not locked. What do you say?"

"I'm not doing that," said Tyrone defiantly.

"Suit yourself. But you better come up with that money soon, boy. And don't come whingeing to me if you lose the game either."

For once it was Tyrone who walked away,

leaving Nick standing at the back of the pavilion with a smile playing on his thin lips. Then his green eyes flashed. The cold hatred in those eyes seemed to come from the depths of his very soul and his body shook for a moment like a quivering, black jelly, before he too walked away.

Tyrone was troubled by the encounter with Nick. What worried him most was that he had been very tempted to steal the money. He desperately wanted to know how to bowl the *wicked* ball that Nick had talked about. It would be all too easy to slip into the umpire's room just before play started. But he wasn't going to do it. He wasn't a thief.

He tried to clear his mind. He would win the game for Vale and no girl batter was going to stand in his way.

As usual, Simon gave him the opening over and let him choose which end he wanted to bowl from. He measured his 18-pace run-up in the shadow of the pavilion, the end from which Cristiano had bowled.

The first ball was a corker and blew away the Jericho opener's middle stump. The stump seemed to hang in the air as if it had been detonated by an explosive…a warning to the ten other batters.

Tyrone felt good: the pain in his groin had nearly gone and he was firing. He watched Jez walk briskly to the wicket, pulling on her gloves and carefully adjusting her helmet strap. She took guard, tapped her bat a couple of times and faced him.

Here's one for Old Nick, you say, half wishing now you didn't have to be reminded of Nick every time you bowl. You steam in and release the ball with a sharp snap of the wrist. The Toe Cruncher is angled into its target at nearly 80mph. It's perfect. Unstoppable. Your arms are already raised in triumph but her bat comes down at the last moment and the ball squirts away for a single. You stare down the pitch in disbelief.

Now you're angry. You fire in a Throat Ball at the other opener. It almost cuts him in two. Then he falls for the Slow Special and his stumps are scattered like skittles. But she is watching you. Like a hawk. She's memorising your tricks, unpicking the secret deliveries. You've already shown her the Toe Cruncher and the Throat Ball and the Reverse-swing Yorker and the Slow Special. Keep something up your sleeve, you tell yourself. She's watching you.

At the end of Tyrone's first over, Jericho Hall were three for 3. His third wicket – a plumb lbw – was followed by a fast lifter to Jez, and she'd

casually picked it off her hips for a single. This girl was good.

She confirmed her class by taking two sweet boundaries off Michael, Vale's other opening bowler and then she ended the over with a cheeky single to keep the strike. She's not afraid, thought Tyrone. She wants to face me.

He tested her with a snorting bouncer. She swayed out of the way of it at the last moment, never taking her eye off the ball.

This girl is making you really angry. You run up and hit the crease hard. It's the fastest delivery you've ever bowled. Must be 80mph...or more? It tucks her up. It's through her defence. But she gets lucky. She's late on her shot but the ball takes the faintest of inside edges and misses the stumps by a hair's breadth. Your head's in your hands. She scampers three runs. "Good ball," she says as she stops at your end.

Two wickets followed in two balls. The first, an lbw, was plumb – a formality for the umpire.

The new batter was the chippy keeper and Tyrone did him with the slow full toss. Had him jumping in the air and took an easy caught-and-bowled off the bat handle. Who's laughing now?

At 15 for five Cristiano walked out to the wicket, facing a hat trick: there were three balls left in the over. Jez came over and had a brief chat with him – it was obvious she was talking about Tyrone. Telling him what was coming.

What was she saying? Ignore them. Keep your mind on the task. You grip the ball for the Fizzer and bound towards the bowling crease. Cristiano stares back at you. Your arm comes over with that perfect surge and you cock your wrist as the ball leaves your hand. It hammers into his pad. But Cristiano is on the front foot...well down the pitch. The umpire shakes his head at your appeal. "Not out," he says. You know he is wrong. You've been robbed of a hat trick.

The next ball beat Cristiano's lunge but bounced just over the bails and the keeper fumbled.

They ran a bye. Jez took another single off the last ball…dabbed down a lifter that was going through like a rocket, and ran. 17 for five.

"Take a break, Tyrone," said Simon.

Take a break! He must be mad. These two will murder the other bowlers.

And so they did.

The Annihilator

It was in the sixth over that Jez really found her timing. First she clipped a half-volley over mid-wicket for four and followed that with an exquisite late cut for another boundary. Cristiano joined in the fun at the other end, chopping Vale's so-called spinner through point. When Jez hit a big six off the same bowler it at last dawned on Simon that he'd have to bring Tyrone back. The score had rattled up to 45 for five.

Tyrone had been fielding on the boundary in front of the pavilion. As the six flew over the boundary, he heard the unmistakable voice of Godfrey Boddy shout, "Fine shot, my girl." And then *God* turned to his neighbour, who was also wearing a blue blazer and tie, and said proudly, "I've signed her up for the County, you know. Reckon she'll be an even bigger star than young Tyrone."

"She seems to have got his measure," said the man in the identical blazer.

We'll see about that, muttered Tyrone to himself.

But Jez had got his mind wobbling. Why else would he have miscounted his run-up at the start of the new spell. 19 instead of 18 paces! The result was a slow half-volley, way outside the off-stump, and Jez was on it like a hawk and smashed it through the covers for four.

He measured out his run again and the next ball was miles better – the *Fizzer* again – but she seemed to read it from his hand and took a long stride down the wicket to smother the back spin. He tried the bouncer, but she ducked out of the way at the last moment. He bowled a cruel out-swinger fired at the stumps and swinging away to the slips, and she watched it and let it pass by harmlessly.

Then something happened that he'd never forget. He bowled another rocket-fast yorker, swinging late into her legs. Jez took half a stride forward and turned the delivery into a low full-toss and her bat came down straight. Then, at the moment of impact, she just turned her top hand and caressed the ball away on the leg side. There was no thwack of leather on willow, no explosion from the blade. The ball was simply eased with precision to the left of the fielder at mid-wicket and to the right of deep mid-on. She had judged its path exactly.

Both fielders set off in pursuit as the ball tracked its way towards the pavilion. The chase was futile. Jez had struck the ball just hard enough to keep the fielders interested, but it raced them to the boundary and won the chase by a couple of metres.

Tyrone stood and watched. And then he looked back at Jez. He would always remember that shot off a good, super-fast delivery as the most beautiful cricket stroke he had ever seen.

Now he was at his wit's end. Jez seemed to be reading all his variations. He'd never bowled at anyone remotely like her. 53 for five. Jez and Cristiano needed a mere 21 runs to win from nine overs. He had to stop one or both of them.

Again Jez got bravely forward and took a sharp lifting ball on the ribs as it jumped at her. It must have hurt, even through the chest protector, but she didn't flinch and ran a leg bye.

Cristiano was now playing almost as well as his batting partner. He was lucky when a thin edge dropped just short of the keeper. But then he dabbed a fast lifter down at his feet and ran a cheeky single off the last ball of the over.

Tyrone trudged out to the boundary to his fielding position, seething with anger. One more over left. One more over to break this partnership or lose the game. Losing to Cristiano was more that he could bear.

Cristiano hit a two over the slips off Simon's bowling and when Jez got on strike she pulled hard and beat Tyrone's run and dive on the mid-wicket boundary.

A wiry little official, wearing a County tracksuit and dark glasses, retrieved the ball. As he handed it to Tyrone his eyes flashed. "Want to change your mind then, boy?" It was Nick.

A chill wind suddenly blew across the ground.

Tyrone shivered. "What's it called, your 'wicked' ball?"

"The *Annihilator*! Shall I show you?"

Tyrone looked around and nodded.

"And the money?"

"I'll get it."

"Nick it?"

"Maybe."

"That's what I like to hear. But you mind you do. Or the wolves and the vultures will come for you. And that's only the beginning of your nightmare if you cheat me." He laughed cruelly and then his voice returned to normal. "Now watch." In the twinkle of an eye, Nick slipped the match ball in his pocket and replaced it with another. It looked identical to Tyrone, but he'd spotted the switch. Nick held the ball with his first two fingers twisted across it. "The secret's in the shoulder – you chuck it instead of bowling it," he said.

"But that's…"

"Illegal, I know. But these umpires will never spot that. No one says much about chucking these days anyhow."

"You've changed the ball."

"Yeah. They won't notice that either. Now get out there and chuck."

"And what will happen?"

"You wait and see. Try and pitch it on a length outside off-stump."

Tyrone returned to the field, under-armed the ball to Simon and then watched Jez hit a perfect cover drive off the final ball of the captain's over. He glanced up at the score board. 66 for five. This is it. Cristiano was facing. This is it. The *Annihilator*.

The ball feels heavy in your hand. Heavier than the old one and slightly smaller. But you're probably just imagining it. You tighten the grip, stare at Cristiano. Feel the surge of anger at the friend who let you down. Here's one for Old Nick. You storm in, hit your front foot down hard and fire. The chuck nearly pulls your shoulder out of its socket.

The ball fizzes audibly in the air like a firework as it leaves your hand... as if it has a life of its own. A split-second later it pitches on a full length. It's already reversing into the batter before it pitches.

He's forward again on the front foot. But the ball leaps like a shot rabbit. Spits off the pitch, gaining pace, gaining venom. It spears in towards him. Hits him on the side of the head. You hear the sickening crack. And he goes down. Your best friend goes down... sinks to his knees and then slumps over on his side. He doesn't move.

Jez was by his side in seconds, telling them not to touch him. Stand back. The bars of the helmet were bent inwards and blood was trickling from the side of Cristiano's head. "Get an ambulance," she said.

One of the umpires ran towards the pavilion. The other called for a stretcher. It came quickly and Cristiano was lifted on to it and carried off. He was still limp. His eyes were open but there was not a flicker of life in them.

Tyrone hadn't moved from the end of his follow-through. He stood as if in a trance, staring at the ball lying on the track by the stumps. "Don't worry, lad," said the umpire. "It wasn't your fault. Nasty delivery, the way it spat up at him.

Must have gone through the top. Not your fault, lad."

Tyrone didn't say a word. Finally he tore his eyes away from the *Annihilator* ball and ran off towards the pavilion. He didn't see the wiry official in the tracksuit and dark glasses pick it up a moment or two later.

A crowd was gathering round the ambulance that had stopped at the back of the pavilion, its engine still running. Tyrone forced his way to the front. The stretcher was being loaded into the back. He couldn't see Cristiano, he was covered with a blanket. Loaded into the ambulance. And then he was gone.

For Thirty Quid

Tyrone didn't stop running till he was a mile or more from the ground. At first he'd run after the ambulance but, of course, it soon disappeared into the distance, its siren screaming. But he kept running. When finally he stopped he realised he was still wearing his cricket whites and his cricket boots. The spikes were sticking into the soft tarmac.

Where was he going? The hospital, of course. He had to find Cristiano. But where was the hospital? He didn't know this part of town. The buildings were unfamiliar: grey-looking residential flats and semi-detached houses.

He wandered about aimlessly for half an hour, maybe more. Then it started to rain and the wind grew stronger. He pressed on against the wind towards the centre of town...or so he thought. The few people about were muffled against the storm. They seemed uncaring, almost alien. Tyrone was sure he saw the eyes of a passer-by flash green as she looked up at him. He kept looking round... convinced Old Nick was on his tail. The wolves and the vultures circling. Voices in his head said: *What are you worrying about? He's no friend of yours.*

Then he stopped and tried to take a grip on himself. This was crazy. The hospital probably wouldn't be in the centre of town anyway. He passed a newsagent's with its light on and went in.

"You look a bit wet, sonny," said the man behind the counter.

"Can you tell me where the hospital is?" asked Tyrone. His voice sounded strained and thin.

"Three miles down the road," said the proprietor, pointing in the direction Tyrone had come from. "You can't miss it."

"Thanks."

"You been playing cricket?"

"Yeah."

"At the county ground?"

Tyrone nodded.

"My boy plays there. You know Ahir Shah?"

"Yeah."

"What you going to the hospital for?"

"My mate got hurt. Gotta find out about him," said Tyrone.

The man looked at him. "You look a bit shook up yourself. And there aren't many buses at this time of day. Tell you what... give me five minutes to lock up and I'll drive you there. Save you getting soaked."

The newsagent introduced himself as "Sachin, same as you know who", as he backed his battered Volvo out of the garage next to his shop.

"You a batter or a bowler?" he asked.

"Bowler."

"What's your name?"

"Tyrone."

"Hey, Tyrone! Ahir never stops talking about you. Says you're the fastest bowler in the county."

Tyrone didn't answer.

"So what happened to your mate?"

"Got hit on the head."

"With a bouncer?"

"Yeah… sort of. And I bowled it."

"Right."

Sachin dropped Tyrone off at reception. "Want me to come with you?" he asked.

"No," said Tyrone. "But thanks."

"You'll get cold in just a cricket shirt. Take this jacket," said Sachin. "It's Ahir's. You can give it back to him any time."

Tyrone nodded a thank you and pulled on the jacket. It fitted him fine.

"Good luck," said Sachin.

A woman wearing steel-rimmed glasses sat at the reception desk. She ignored Tyrone for a full three minutes as she typed something into her computer. Then she looked piercingly at him over the top of her glasses. "Name?"

Tyrone told her his name and she tapped away at the computer again.

"No one here of that name."

Tyrone explained and she looked him up and down as if he was a Martian. He told her Cristiano's name.

Accident & Emergency

"Just admitted from A&E. He's in ENT for tests," she said.

"What's ENT?"

She ignored him.

"Where is it, please? ENT?"

"Second floor. Partridge Wing. But you can't go there."

"But I'm his friend," said Tyrone.

"Family only. Come tomorrow at visiting time."

"Is he all right?"

The woman sighed. "Ask over there. Patient

Information. Next!" She dismissed him with a toss of her head.

There was no one at the Patient Information desk so Tyrone took the lift up to the second floor.

A nurse on the ENT desk stopped him as he walked into the ward. "What can I do for you, honey?" she said.

"What's ENT?" asked Tyrone.

"Ear, Nose and Throat," said the nurse with a smile.

"I'd like to see my…brother," said Tyrone, giving her Cristiano's name.

"Let's see," said the nurse. "Well, he's not supposed to have visitors. He's got concussion, you know."

"Concussion?"

"He took a nasty blow to the head… with a cricket ball, I think. He was unconscious for over an hour."

"He's OK?" said Tyrone in a nervous, quiet voice.

"He'll be fine," said the nurse with a smile. The phone rang and she answered it and listened to the caller's enquiry. "He's perfectly all right," she said eventually. "Just a bit of concussion and a nasty cut. We've stitched him up and we're keeping him in over night for tests on his eardrum. But I don't believe there's any damage." She listened again. "Right," she said and was about to put down the phone when she added. "Listen, his brother's here. Do you want to speak to your son?"

Another short silence. Tyrone tried to shuffle from foot to foot but his spikes had got stuck in the lino.

"What?" She looked at Tyrone sternly. "Cristiano's father says he hasn't got a brother!"

"Tell him it's Tyrone," said Tyrone.

After Tyrone had fully explained why he'd lied and who he was and how Cristiano had got injured, the nurse accepted his story and she allowed him to see his friend... though "only for a couple of minutes, mind."

Cristiano had a big bandage across his ear and the side of his face was swollen and purple and yellow and red. As he looked at what he'd done, Tyrone was at first too shocked to speak.

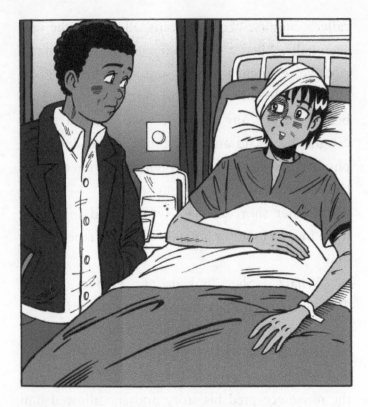

Cristiano tried to smile at his friend and winced with pain. "I keep forgetting I shouldn't smile," he said.

"Sorry," said Tyrone quietly.

"Wasn't your fault."

"It was."

"How?"

"I'll tell you when you're better."

"OK, I'll hold you to that. It was a hell of a ball... but did you chuck it?"

"Yes."

"Are we still friends?"

"I wouldn't want me for a friend if I were you."

"Don't be stupid," said Cristiano, wincing again as he tried to smile.

"OK, that's enough, *brother*," said the nurse. As they left, she turned to Cristiano. "Your dad will be here soon." And she added, "He says he'll give you a lift home afterwards, Tyrone."

Sharp Turn

Tyrone knew it was only a matter of time before he saw Old Nick again.

He was alone at the cricket nets. He'd come to think... and to practise his new bowling action. It wasn't working out too well. For the third time, the ball looped on to the top of the nets and he had to knock it down with a stick.

"You're pretty crap at that, aren't you?" said the familiar voice.

Tyrone didn't reply.

"What are you trying to do, anyway?" said Old Nick.

"Bowl leg-breaks."

"And what's wrong with bowling fast?"

"I think I'll be better at leg-breaks."

"OK. What you do is you come off six paces and you say…"

"No."

"What you mean, 'No'?"

"I mean I don't need your help. I'm going to do it my way."

"The crap way?"

"If you like."

"You're making a big mistake, Tyrone."

"I don't think so."

Old Nick smiled his self-satisfied smile. "So what about the money? I want it, you know. And now."

Tyrone dug his hand into his pocket and proffered Nick a roll of three ten-pound notes.

"Where'd you get that from? Did you steal it?"

"No, my mum gave it to me. I've got to pay her back."

"But that's stupid. You don't need to…."

"Yes I do," said Tyrone firmly. "Now will you go away, please? There's someone over there, coming to see me."

And there he was… Cristiano, walking towards

them across the playing fields. They both watched him for a moment and, when Tyrone turned back to speak to Nick, the little man had done one of his vanishing tricks. But as usual he had the last word.

"Fool!" was all he said. Just one syllable, but never was a single sound so full of bitterness and anger and scorn.

"Who was that talking to you?" asked Cristiano, greeting his friend with a big grin.

"Just some weirdo," said Tyrone. "What you doing here?" He gave his friend a slap on the back.

Cristiano winced. "Careful, I'm still a bit sore. I thought I'd come over to show you my scars and my black eye. Your mum said you were practising on your own. There's a surprise!"

Tyrone had visited Cristiano again in hospital and gone to see him twice at home after he was let out of hospital. But this was the first time he'd seen him without his bandages. The black-and-purple bruise wrapped round his face from his ear to his nose, and a livid wound on the side of his head was held together with butterfly plasters.

Tyrone tried to tell his friend for the hundredth time that the ball he'd bowled was dangerous, that he'd chucked it, that it was no accident and he'd been trying to hurt him.

But Cristiano wouldn't listen. "What's the problem, Ty?" he said. "I was too slow. I should have got my head out of the way. And there's no damage... just a few stitches. It was an accident, right?"

An accident! Tyrone knew he could have killed Cristiano. He knew he'd got that close to ending his friend's life just to win a cricket game. Just to prove he was the best fast bowler in the county. The *deadliest* fast bowler.

He'd told his mum about Old Nick... said Nick had been coaching him and he owed him £30 in fees. She said it was disgraceful, taking advantage of young kids and she wanted to tell Nick what she thought of him.

But Tyrone persuaded her against it. He told her he wanted to put it behind him and forget about Nick forever. He'd get a part-time job and pay her back. And finally she agreed.

And now, at last, it was over. He'd seen the last of Old Nick.

"Let's see you bowl," said Cristiano. "Show me how you do that reverse swinging yorker."

"No, I'm not bowling fast any more. I'm trying to bowl leg-breaks."

"Spin? Why? But you're the best fast bowler in the…"

"Not any more… I'm going to be a spinner," said Tyrone with a look that left no room for argument. "Only I can't seem to get the grip right. Can you show me how you do it?"

"Well, OK." Cristiano took the taped-up tennis ball and demonstrated how he should hold it. Fingers splayed. He showed Tyrone the leg-break wrist action. "You need a lot of power in the shoulder to get it to come out right. I usually flick it off the ring finger, like this." He bowled the ball and Tyrone retrieved it.

"Right," said Tyrone. "Watch this."

He ran in off seven paces, aimed down the pitch, with his left elbow lifted high, and bowled. The ball wobbled a little in the air, hit the mat on a good length just outside the leg stump and spun in sharply to hit the plank.

"Hey! See that turn?" said Cristiano with a smile. "Not bad, Ty. You could be right. Keep practising and you could be better than Shane Warne one day. And you should get that manager of yours to find you a bowling coach."

"What manager?"

"The little bald one."

"Oh, you mean Godfrey Boddy."

"Yeah, that's the one. He knows everyone, doesn't he?"

Tyrone shrugged.

"Did you know he tried to sign Jez up?" said Cristiano.

"I haven't heard from him since... since that game," said Tyrone.

"Well, we'll still have to find you a spin-bowling coach. It's as competitive as hell getting to the top, you know."

"Yes," said Tyrone with a weak smile. "I know."

ABOUT 'CHANCE TO SHINE
SUPPORTED BY BRIT INSURANCE'

'Chance to Shine supported by Brit Insurance' is one of the biggest grass-roots sport for development programmes ever undertaken in Britain. The Cricket Foundation charity runs Chance to Shine and aims to establish regular coaching and competitive cricket opportunities in a third of state schools by 2015. As a result, two million primary and secondary children will reap the educational benefits of playing competitive cricket.

The programme now links nearly 4,000 schools to 500 local cricket clubs, through County Boards, and qualified cricket coaches provide up to 280 hours coaching and competition to a cluster of eight primary and two secondary schools. Chance to Shine projects receive a maximum of five years' funding to achieve a level of sustainable, competitive cricket. Great emphasis is placed on competition, the 'migration' of children from schools to clubs and teacher training to ensure that cricket cultures continue in schools post Chance to Shine.

To find out more about Chance to Shine,
visit the website: chancetoshine.org

BOB CATTELL has been a cricket fan all his life
and a supporter of the England team through
thick and thin. He also supports Yorkshire,
especially for their fast bowlers
from Fred Trueman to Tim Bresnan.

He is the author of the bestselling *Glory Gardens*
series about cricket, highly recommended by
TestMatch Special, and the *Strikers* series
about football, written with David Ross.
He also wrote the *Butter-Finger* cricket books for
Frances Lincoln, with John Agard: *Butter-Finger*,
Shine on, Butter-Finger and *Big City Butter-Finger*
("hugely entertaining" – Carousel).

Bob describes his own cricketing abilities
as 'a left-arm spin bowler who surprises batters
with the lack of spin'. He lives in Suffolk.

BUTTER-FINGER
Bob Cattell and John Agard
Illustrated by Pam Smy

Riccardo Small may not be a great cricketer – he's only
played twice before for *Calypso Cricket Club* – but he's
mad about the game and can tell you the averages of every
West Indies cricketer in history. His other love is writing
calypsos. Today is Riccardo's chance to make his mark with
Calypso CC against The Saints. The game goes right down
to the wire with captain, Natty, and team-mates Bashy and
Leo striving for victory, but then comes the moment that
changes everything for Riccardo…

SHINE ON, BUTTER-FINGER
Bob Cattell and John Agard
Illustrated by Pam Smy

Calypso and cricket come together in the Island's Carnival,
and Riccardo has to choose between his two passions.
He has been invited to sing at the annual Calypso Final,
competing against the most famous singers on the Island,
and amidst the pan bands, the masqueraders and the
stick-fighters he discovers why the singing competition
is called 'Calypso War'. Meanwhile his team-mates at
Calypso Cricket Club are playing the most important game
in their history and their new captain, Bashy has a lot
to learn in a very short time...

BIG CITY BUTTER-FINGER
Bob Cattell and John Agard
Illustrated by Pam Smy

"Three thousand seats and every one sold out.
Three thousand people watch you sing, Butter-Finger!"

Fame has come early for Riccardo. He's in the big city, far
away from his Island home, and starring at the London
Caribbean Festival, under his stage name, Butter-Finger.
But his performance in front of a huge, devoted audience is
brought to a halt by a single face in the crowd. And this
chance encounter throws Riccardo's whole life into turmoil.

Meanwhile Riccardo's friends at *Calypso Cricket Club* are
facing their biggest test by far. Complete outsiders in the
celebrated Valentine Shield tournament in Trinidad, they are
playing for the reputation of the Island, under the spotlight
of the whole West Indian cricketing world…

"Glorious delight in words. Great fun!" –
School Librarian